DOLLS AND TRUCKS ARE FOR EVERYONE

Written by
ROBB PEARLMAN

Illustrated by
EDA KABAN

author and illustrator of *Pink Is for Boys*

RP|KIDS
PHILADELPHIA

Running Press Kids
Hachette Book Group
1290 Avenue of the Americas, New York, NY 10104
www.runningpress.com/rpkids
@RP_Kids

Printed in China

First Edition: September 2021

Published by Running Press Kids, an imprint of Perseus Books, LLC,
a subsidiary of Hachette Book Group, Inc. The Running Press Kids name and logo
is a trademark of the Hachette Book Group.

The Hachette Speakers Bureau provides a wide range of authors for speaking events.
To find out more, go to www.hachettespeakersbureau.com or call (866) 376-6591.

The publisher is not responsible for websites (or their content)
that are not owned by the publisher.

Print book cover and interior design by Frances J. Soo Ping Chow.

Library of Congress Control Number: 2020930890

ISBNs: 978-0-7624-7156-0 (hardcover), 978-0-7624-7154-6 (ebook),
978-0-7624-7211-6 (ebook), 978-0-7624-7210-9 (ebook)

1010

10 9 8 7 6 5 4 3 2 1

THIS BOOK IS FOR WALT.
—R. P.

TO ŞEBO.
WELCOME TO THE FAMILY!
—E. K.

Dolls and trucks are for everyone.

Toys are for boys and girls

and anyone who wants to play.

Capes and scrubs are for heroes:
girls, boys, and everyone who wants to help.

Dancing shoes are for boys, girls, and everyone.

Anyone can dance, dance, dance!

Fabric and wood
are for everyone:

boys, girls, and anyone
who wants to create.

Hockey and figure skating are for girls, boys, and everyone.

Ice rinks are fun for anyone who wants to gliiiide and sliiiiiide and spin, spin, spin.

Whisks and spoons are for anyone
who wants to lick the bowl.

Flutes and drums are for boys, girls, and everyone.

Music is for anyone who wants to share a song.

Unicorns are for anyone because . . . **unicorns!!**

Video games and books are for girls, boys,
and everyone.

Adventure is for anyone
who loves a good story.

Robots are for puppies.

Well, *maybe* not puppies.
But they are for anyone who wants to code.

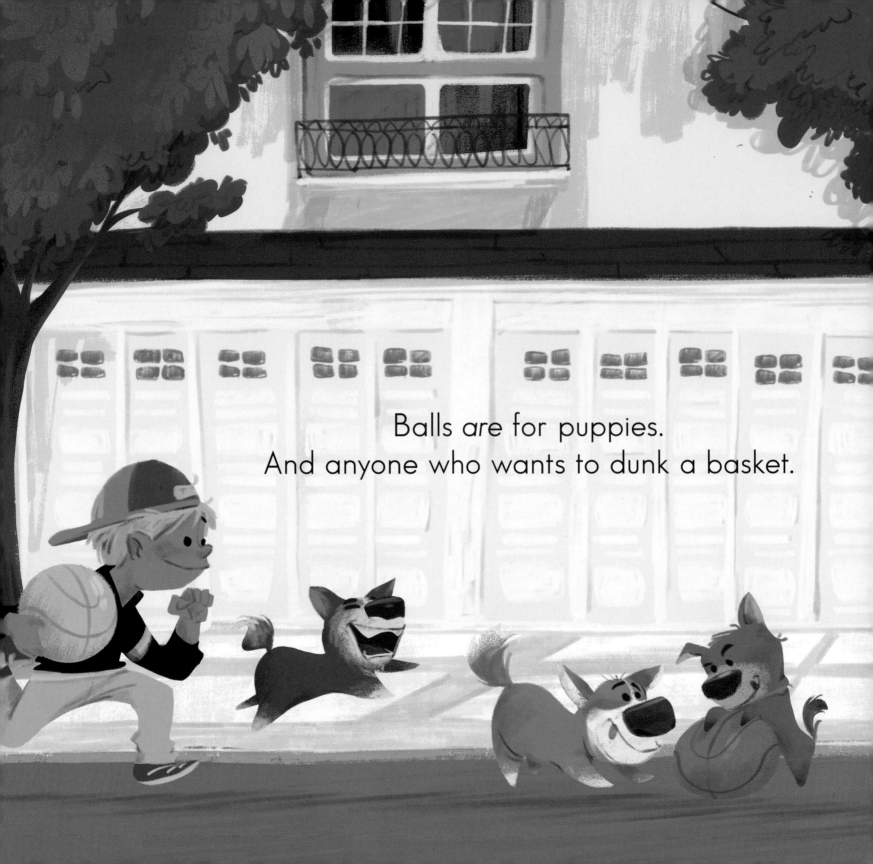

Balls are for puppies.
And anyone who wants to dunk a basket.

Gardens and farms are for boys, girls,
and everyone.

Anyone can get their hands dirty!

Listening and kindness are for kids
and grown-ups

and anyone who wants
to learn and grow.

You are for me and I am for you

and anyone you want to be.

A boy, a girl, whoever you are.